This book is dedicated to my amazing children Joshua and Alyssa. It is by their example of courage to take flight and be adventurous in life, that has given me the confidence to make my dream of writing a book come true.

I'd like to acknowledge my dad, Adolfo Quezada, for editing this book and sharing his wealth of knowledge on his favorite subject, hummingbirds. I'm forever grateful to have shared this project with him.

"Hey, you stay away from my babies!" a hummingbird poked at a hungry hawk who had approached her nest. She was on guard, protecting herself and her tiny eggs that would soon turn into tiny hummingbirds.

"Ouch!" squawked the hawk as he backed off. "For such a tiny bird, you sure are courageous," he said as he flew away.

"You messed with the wrong Momma," she chirped and sat on her eggs to keep them warm.
"I will never let anything hurt you," Momma spoke to her little ones, who were still inside their eggs. "One day soon you will hatch from your shells. Every day you will grow and learn about life; then, someday you will be strong enough to start your own journey. But until then, I will protect you and teach you everything I know."

From within my shell, I could hear Momma talking to us. I was so ready to meet her and my brother. Tap, tap, tap, crack. Tap, tap, tap, crack. I cracked a sliver in my shell and I sensed brightness coming from the outside. Tap, tap, tap, CRACK! I broke through my shell completely. I shook it away, yawned, and felt the fresh spring air on my back.

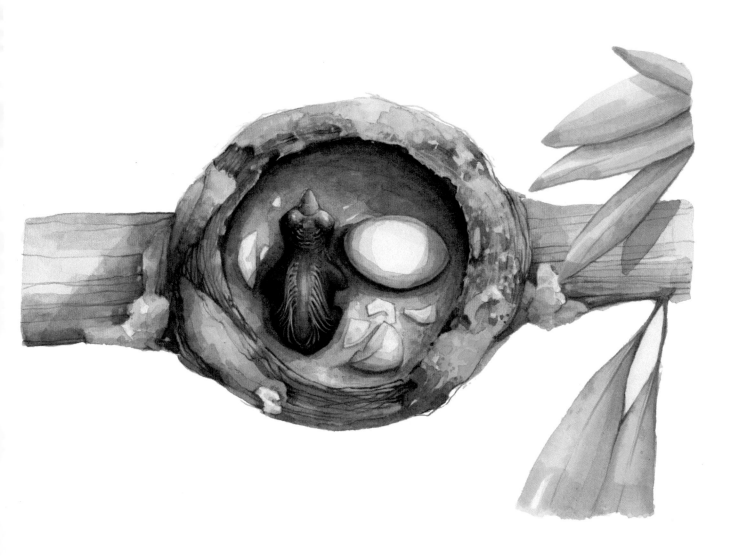

Soon after, my brother hatched too. We snuggled each other. And although we could not see clearly yet, Momma welcomed us with her tender voice, "Hello, my sweet babies. Welcome to the world." She nourished us with the nectar and insects she had stored in her throat for us. We felt her love immediately.

We slept a lot in the beginning of life. Momma ventured out to collect food for us while we stayed quiet and still. We didn't want to be seen by a hungry hawk or anything else that could hurt us.

We heard the hum of Momma's wings when she returned. We heard sounds from all around us. Momma told us the sounds were the music of the world. I wondered what the world was? My curiosity grew.

After a few weeks, our eyes were finally opened. Momma perched on the edge of our nest. She was so beautiful. Her feathers gleamed like jewels in the sunlight. Momma gave us each a name: I would be called Hope, and my brother was Henry.

Momma took every chance to teach us about life. She told us where and how to gather our food, warned us of those who might want to hurt us, and told us how to protect ourselves from danger. "Never be afraid to stand up for yourself," she declared.

She told us about the great adventures of migration flights across the world. Henry flapped his wings in excitement. "I'm going to fly 500 miles!" he announced.

"How exciting," said Momma, "but not all at once. All that flying needs plenty of rest and food to reserve your strength and energy."

Momma also told us stories about the beautiful yards she had explored. They were arrayed with nectar-filled flowers, feeders filled with delicious sugar water, and friendly people who loved hummingbirds. That sounded like the good life to me.

One night Momma said, "Someday, you will be ready to fly away from our nest. Remember, I will always be around for you." Momma kissed our foreheads and told us that she loved us. We fell asleep under her warmth, the moon and the stars. I dreamt about my journey through life.

The day came when Henry and I were grown up enough to learn how to fly. Momma promised to stay nearby until we were safely on our own. I perched on the edge of our nest. I stretched and fluffed my feathers. I felt excited and a little nervous. "I don't want to fall," said Henry as he worked up his courage. "You go first," he said. "Let's try together," we agreed.

I jumped onto a nearby branch. Henry joined me. We explored different branches in our tree. We got better and better at flying. Momma was there encouraging us. Suddenly, Henry flapped his wings so fast that he took flight. "Weee, I'm flying! I'm flying!" he exclaimed. We clapped our wings and cheered for him.

Henry loved flying! "Look what I can do!" he said as he flew backward. Then he dove forward and flew upside down.

Now it was my turn. I gave it a whirl. I zigged and zagged. I circled Henry. "Woohoo, this is fun! Look mom! We're flying!"

Momma led us from flower to flower to find food to keep our energy up. We found insects too. We practiced so much that we were exhausted. We perched on a branch to rest and soon were sleeping deeply.

The next morning, I woke up and looked around. The world was quiet. Momma was gone and that meant it was time. "Henry, are you awake?" I asked.

"Yup," he yawned. "Today is the day, Hope. I'm ready to start my journey." I'm going to journey out and see the world!"

"You're going to have a great adventure, Henry," I told him. "I'm going to find the most beautiful yard and build a nest of my own. I will have babies of my own someday just like Momma. We will visit her all the time and you will tell us about your great adventures."

"Ready?" I asked.

"Ready!" Henry answered. We wrapped our wings around each other. "See you soon," we both promised. Henry took off first. He stopped midair, turned toward me and did a somersault.

Then he waved his wings and flew into the wild blue yonder.

"Show off!" I giggled and headed out in search of my new home.

I found a beautiful yard to call home. I perched on a branch nestled in an inviting Mesquite tree. It felt safe and secure. I slept in peace and quiet. Each morning, I heard a door open, then human footsteps and whistling.

It was Charlie, the owner of the yard. He watered the grass and the flowers. Then he filled the hummingbird feeder. Finally, he spoke to me, "Good morning, Hope."

I hovered in place in front of him and chirped, "Good morning, Charlie."

Before I met Charlie, he was lonely and sad. He stayed indoors thinking about his wife, who had died recently. But then I came along and changed his life, or so he told me. He had seen me through the window and came outside to greet me.

"Well, aren't you a beautiful sight," Charlie said. "Welcome to my yard. Please stay as long as you want." We became good friends. He told me that he was glad I was there and that I had given him hope again.

I'm glad I chose to live in Charlie's yard. I can hear the sounds of the world. I drink nectar from his feeder and from his many-splendid flowers. I venture out to visit Momma and Henry when he's in town, but mostly I stay here. I love it here. In fact, it's such a pleasant place for me that I plan to build a nest like Momma built.

I will piece together the tiniest twigs, spiderweb fiber, bits of leaves, and a string or two to make it strong enough to hold my babies. I will protect them from danger and teach them everything I know about life. They will come and they will go; and I will love them forever.

Made in the USA
Middletown, DE
15 February 2022

61214187R00018